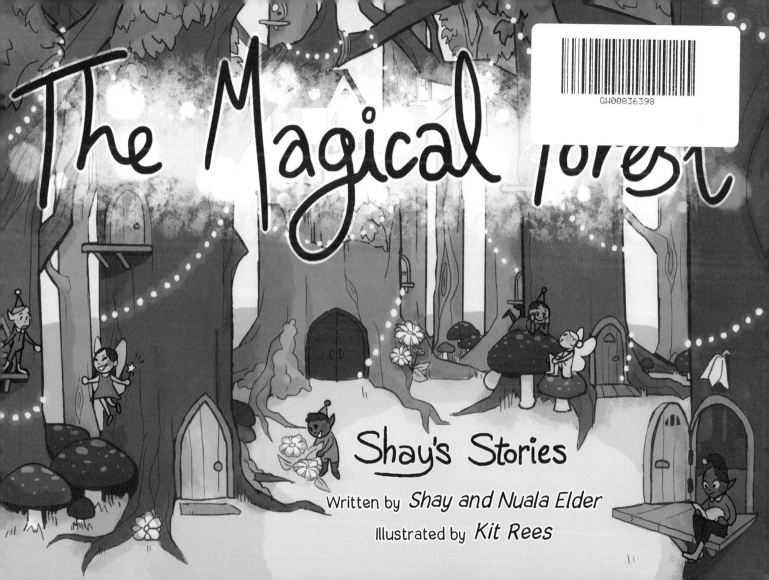

The Magical Forest

Shay's Stories

Written by **Shay and Nuala Elder**

Illustrated by **Kit Rees**

This book is dedicated to my family
(Daddy, Mummy, Eve, Amy and Alex),
to my Granny and Granda Gault and
Aunty Tara.

Lots of Love, from Shay

The Magical Forest by Shay Elder © 2019

The Magical Forest

Written by

Shay and Nuala Elder

About the authors: Shay and his mummy Nuala loved making up stories that rhymed when Shay was a little boy. Shay has autism and loved the rhymes and making up the stories with his mum and now that he is grown up he wants to share all his stories with children everywhere!

Illustrated by

Kit Rees

Find Kit's work at *kitrees.com*

There is a *magical forest* not very far away,

Where magic happens every night and every single day

the fairy dust sparkles brightly high up in the sky

And lots of pretty fairy lights twinkle in your eye.

Santa's elves come here for holidays
to have a little break.

After building toys for Christmas, a little rest they take.

And naughty little pixies  meet up to make a plan

To see what tricks they will play on anyone they can

Where Tooth Fairies gently sleep after collecting children's teeth

snuggled inside a magic tree under a cosy leaf

So if you visit The
Magical Forest,

be as quiet
as can be...

As you might see a fairy flying home to her little tree

Or maybe see a busy elf who is  working planting seeds

Or catch a naughty pixie getting up to naughty deeds

It's magical in the forest, a special place to go

With lots to see or do in summer, rain or snow.

THE END

This page is brought to you by *Eimhear Kenny, aged 12*, for Shay's Stories.

Eimhear plans to become an author and illustrator when she is older and this is her first published picture.

Keep an eye out for more books from **Shay's Stories!**

Upcoming:

My Red Jumper

How Much Does Mummy Love Me

Ants in my Pants

At the Beach

And many more!

Shay's Stories

Printed in Great Britain
by Amazon